Story Time with Signs & Rhymes

Famous Fenton Has a Farm
Sign Language for Farm Animals

by Dawn Babb Prochovnic
illustrated by Stephanie Bauer

Content Consultant:
William Vicars, EdD, Director of Lifeprint Institute
and Associate Professor, ASL & Deaf Studies
California State University, Sacramento

magic
Wagon

visit us at www.abdopublishing.com

For my parents, who surrounded me with books when I was a child — DP
For Bella, Reid, and Adrian — SB

Published by Magic Wagon, a division of the ABDO Group, 8000 West 78th Street, Edina, Minnesota 55439.

Printed in the United States.

♲ PRINTED ON RECYCLED PAPER

Written by Dawn Babb Prochovnic
Illustrations by Stephanie Bauer
Edited by Stephanie Hedlund and Rochelle Baltzer
Cover and Interior layout and design by Neil Klinepier

Story Time with Signs & Rhymes provides an introduction to ASL vocabulary through stories that are written and structured in English. ASL is a separate language with its own structure. Just as there are personal and regional variations in spoken and written languages, there are similar variations in sign language.

Library of Congress Cataloging-in-Publication Data

Prochovnic, Dawn Babb.
  Famous Fenton has a farm : sign language for farm animals / by Dawn Babb Prochovnic ; illustrated by Stephanie Bauer ; content consultant, William Vicars.
    p. cm. -- (Story time with signs & rhymes)
  Includes "alphabet handshapes;" American Sign Language glossary, fun facts, and activities; further reading and web sites.
  ISBN 978-1-60270-669-9
  [1. Stories in rhyme. 2. Domestic animals--Fiction. 3. American Sign Language. 4. Vocabulary.] I. Bauer, Stephanie, ill. II. Title.
  PZ8.3.P93654Fam 2009
  [E]--dc22

2009002442

Alphabet Handshapes

American Sign Language (ASL) is a visual language that uses handshapes, movements, and facial expressions. Sometimes people spell English words by making the handshape for each letter in the word they want to sign. This is called fingerspelling. The pictures below show the handshapes for each letter in the manual alphabet.

Famous Fenton has a farm. Yee ha hee ha ho!
And on that farm are famous **pets**. Yee ha hee ha ho!
There are many **pets** that you won't forget.
Silly **pets**, frilly **pets**, have you met these **pets** yet?
Famous Fenton has a farm. Yee ha hee ha ho!

pet

5

And on that farm are famous **pigs**. Yee ha hee ha ho!
There are two big **pigs** wearing pink **pig** wigs.
Singing **pigs**, swinging **pigs**, dancing fancy **pig** jigs.
Famous Fenton has a farm. Yee ha hee ha ho!

pig

And on that farm are famous **COWS**. Yee ha hee ha ho!
There's a **COW** that bows and a **COW** that meows.
Happy **COWS**, sappy **COWS**, trading joyful **COW** vows.
Famous Fenton has a farm. Yee ha hee ha ho!

COW

9

And on that farm are famous **ducks**. Yee ha hee ha ho!
There are daring **ducks** racing pickup trucks.
Flapping **ducks**, clapping **ducks**, one excited **duck** clucks.
Famous Fenton has a farm. Yee ha hee ha ho!

duck

And on that farm are famous **goats**. Yee ha hee ha ho!
There are **goats** in boats and a **goat** that floats.
Splashy **goats**, flashy **goats**, zipped in shiny **goat** coats.
Famous Fenton has a farm. Yee ha hee ha ho!

goat

And on that farm are famous **crows**. Yee ha hee ha ho!
There are rows of **crows** wearing bright **crow** bows.
Classy **crows**, sassy **crows**, waving painted **crow** toes.
Famous Fenton has a farm. Yee ha hee ha ho!

crow

And on that farm are famous **dogs**. Yee ha hee ha ho!
There are **dogs** in clogs chasing playful frogs.
Chunky **dogs**, spunky **dogs**, out on zany **dog** jogs.
Famous Fenton has a farm. Yee ha hee ha ho!

or

dog

17

And on that farm are famous **cats**. Yee ha hee ha ho!
There are big fat **cats** swinging baseball bats.
Running **cats**, sunning **cats**, wearing sporty **cat** hats.
Famous Fenton has a farm. Yee ha hee ha ho!

cat

And on that farm are famous **mice**. Yee ha hee ha ho!
There are **mice** on ice, spinning once then twice.
Twirly **mice**, whirly **mice**, skating really nice **mice**.
Famous Fenton has a farm. Yee ha hee ha ho!

mouse

And on that farm are famous **sheep**. Yee ha hee ha ho!
There are **sheep** that leap over **sheep** five deep.
Jumping **sheep**, bumping **sheep**, bouncing off to **sheep** sleep.
Famous Fenton has a farm. Yee ha hee ha ho!

sheep

And now you've met Fenton's famous pets. Yee ha hee ha ho!
Oh, there's one last pet that you've not yet met.
Slipping pet, tripping pet, now she's with the pet vet.
Famous Fenton has a farm. Yee ha hee ha ho!

horse

It's so much fun at Fenton's **farm**!
Yee ha hee ha ho!
See you soon at Fenton's **farm**.
Yee ha hee ha ho!

farm

American Sign Language Glossary

cat: Move your "F Hand" from the side of your mouth and out. It should look like you are making cat whiskers.

cow: Touch the thumb of your "Y Hand" to the side of your head near your eyebrow and gently twist your hand forward and back. It should look like you are making the horn of a cow.

crow: Fingerspell C-R-O-W. Or you can use the sign for bird. To sign bird, point your "G Hand" in front of your mouth and open and close your pointer finger and your thumb two times. It should look like you are showing a bird opening and closing its beak.

or

dog: Snap your fingers twice. Another way to sign dog is to pat your hand against the side of your leg a couple of times. It should look like you are calling a dog.

duck: Put your hand in front of your mouth with your first two fingers and your thumb pointing out. Now open and close your fingers and your thumb two times. It should look like you are showing a duck opening and closing its bill.

farm: Touch the thumb of your "Five Hand" to your chin, then drag your thumb across your chin. It should look like you are showing the beard of a farmer.

goat: Make a bent "V Hand" and touch your chin, then quickly touch the top of your forehead. It should look like you are showing a goat's beard and horns.

 **horse:** Touch the thumbs of your "U Hand" to the sides of your head near your eyebrows, and gently bend your first two fingers forward and back. It should look like you are showing the ears of a horse flap back and forth.

 mouse: Gently brush your pointer finger across the tip of your nose twice. It should look like you are showing the twitchy nose of a mouse.

 **pet:** Gently rub your right hand across the back of your left hand. It should look like you are gently petting an animal.

 **pig:** Place your hand under your chin and bend your fingers back and forth at the knuckles. It should look like you are showing a pig's snout poking around in the mud.

 **sheep:** Put your left arm in front of your body. Move your right "V Hand" like a pair of scissors across the top of your left arm. It should look like you are trimming the wool from a sheep.

Fun Facts about ASL

If you know you are going to repeat a fingerspelled word during a conversation or story, you can fingerspell it the first time, then quickly show a related ASL sign to use when the word comes up again. For example, you can fingerspell C-R-O-W, then sign "bird." This shows your signing partner that you mean "crow" the next time you sign "bird."

Most sign language dictionaries describe how a sign looks for a right-handed signer. If you are left-handed, you would modify the instructions so the signs feel more comfortable to you. For example, to sign "sheep," a left-handed signer would hold the right arm in front of the body and use the left "V Hand" to show the "scissors" trimming the sheep's wool.

Signing is fun to learn and can be helpful in many ways. Kids who sign often become better readers and stronger spellers than kids who don't sign. Even babies can learn to use sign language to communicate before they can talk. And when you learn to sign, you can communicate with many people who are deaf.

Signing Activities

Play "I Spy": Get a piece of construction paper, some old magazines, scissors, and paste. Find and cut out pictures from the magazines. Be sure to include pictures for the animals that are mentioned in the story. Paste pictures to the construction paper until your entire page is full. Once your collage is finished, find a partner to play "I Spy." Start with, "I spy with my little eye," and show the sign for an animal from the story. Your partner should search your collage for that animal. Take turns giving clues and searching for pictures until you have practiced the signs for each animal.

Sign Language Guessing Game: This is a fun game for partners. Take turns being the signer. The first signer makes the sign for one of the animals mentioned in the story. The partner makes the sound for the animal that was signed. When the partner makes the correct sound, switch roles. Continue taking turns until you and your partner have correctly made the signs and sounds for each animal mentioned in the story.

Advanced Guessing Game Challenge: This game is similar to the game above, but it requires more practice. In this game, partners take turns being the signer and the fingerspeller. The first signer makes the sign for one of the animals mentioned in the story. The partner fingerspells the word for the animal that was signed. When the partner correctly fingerspells the word that was signed, switch roles.

Additional Resources

Further Reading

Costello, Elaine, PhD. *Random House Webster's Concise American Sign Language Dictionary*. Bantam, 2002.

Heller, Lora. *Sign Language for Kids*. Sterling, 2004.

Sign2Me. *Pick Me Up! Fun Songs for Learning Signs (A CD and Activity Guide)*. Northlight Communications, 2003.

Warner, Penny. *Signing Fun*. Gallaudet University Press, 2006.

Web Sites

To learn more about ASL, visit ABDO Group online at **www.abdopublishing.com**. Web sites about ASL are featured on our Book Links page. These links are routinely monitored and updated to provide the most current information available.